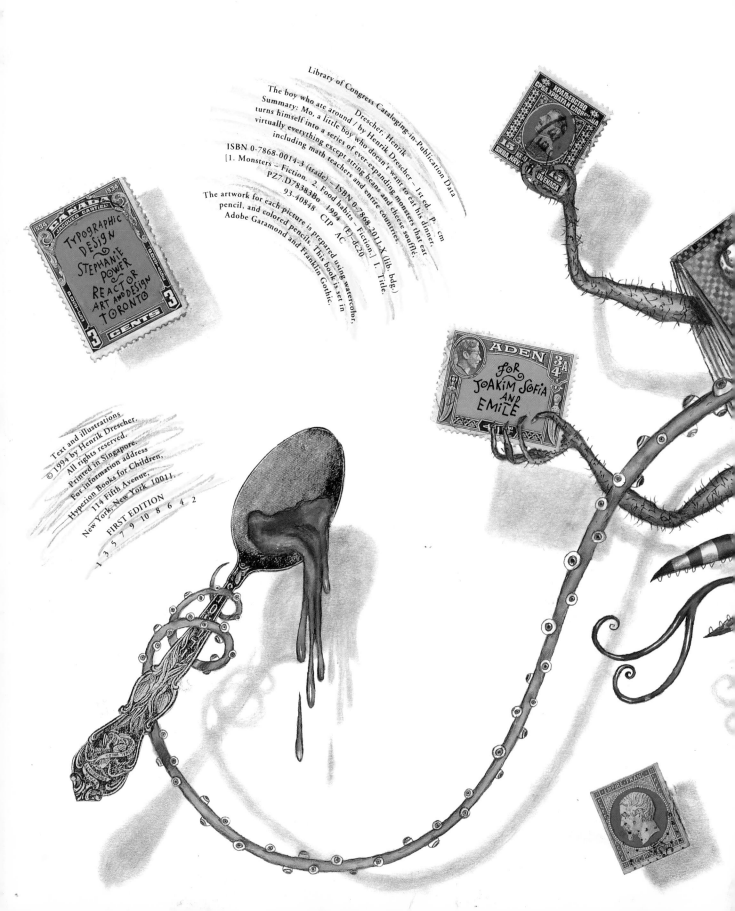

Library of Congress Cataloging-in-Publication Data

Drescher, Henrik
The boy who ate around / by Henrik Drescher – 1st ed. p. cm
Summary: Mo, a little boy who doesn't want to eat his dinner,
turns himself into a series of ever-expanding monsters that eat
virtually everything except string beans and cheese soufflé,
including math teachers and entire countries.
ISBN 0-7868-0014-3 (trade) – ISBN 0-7868-2011-X (lib. bdg.)
[1. Monsters – Fiction. 2. Food habits – Fiction.] I. Title.
PZ7.D78383Bo 1994 (E)–dc20
93-40848 CIP AC

The artwork for each picture is prepared using watercolor,
pencil, and colored pencils. This book is set in
Adobe Garamond and Franklin Gothic.

TYPOGRAPHIC
DESIGN
STEPHANIE
POWER
REACTOR
ART AND DESIGN
TORONTO

FIRST EDITION
1 3 5 7 9 10 8 6 4 2

FOR
JOAKIM SOFIA
AND
EMILE

THE BOY WHO ATE AROUND

HENRIK DRESCHER

HYPERION BOOKS FOR CHILDREN, NEW YORK

There once was a boy named **Mo** who had to **eat his dinner** even though he **didn't** like it **one** little **bit.**

He took a bite of the **lizard** guts and **bullfrog** heads

(ACTUALLY STRING BEANS AND CHEESE SOUFFLÉ)

and *felt* like THROWING IT all up, right there on the dinner TABLE, but he was polite and DIDN'T. INSTEAD, he decided to eat around it.

green wart**hog**

monster

his MoM and DaD.

MUNCHY!)

Then he **ate** the table and chairs. (CRUNCHY!)

The cars were greasy, the **house** was chewy.
(THE PLUMBING STUCK IN HIS THROAT LIKE FISH BONES.)

Next he swallowed the neighbor's cat, followed by the neighbor and his wife.

When there was **no more** room left in the **belly** of the warthog monster,

he changed into something more comfortable—

a very **large** scaly *pink-eyed* **alligator chirper —**

and proceeded to **devour** his school, kids and all.

His **math teacher** he **saved** for last. (YUCK!!!)

To get the bad taste out of his mouth, he ate his best friend, Theo.

He then **munched** down the **rest** of the **town**,

His belly was now **tight** as a **drum** with **all** that **was** in it,

the **mall**, and city hall.

so he changed into a **humongous** bug-eyed **Slime slusher**

the President,

the First Lady,

and ate the White House,

First Dog,

and

First Frog.

(WARTY!)

After which he devoured the whole country, state by state. Every town and

WASHINGTON
OREGON
IDAHO
MONTANA
N. DAKOTA
MINNESOTA
NEVADA
WYOMING
S. DAKOTA
NEBRASKA
MISSOURI
UTAH
COLORADO
KANSAS
ARIZONA
NEW MEXICO
OKLAHOMA
ARKAN
TEXAS
MASS.
VT. N.H.
CONN. R.I.

The East he dipped into the Great Salt Lake. The North he peppered

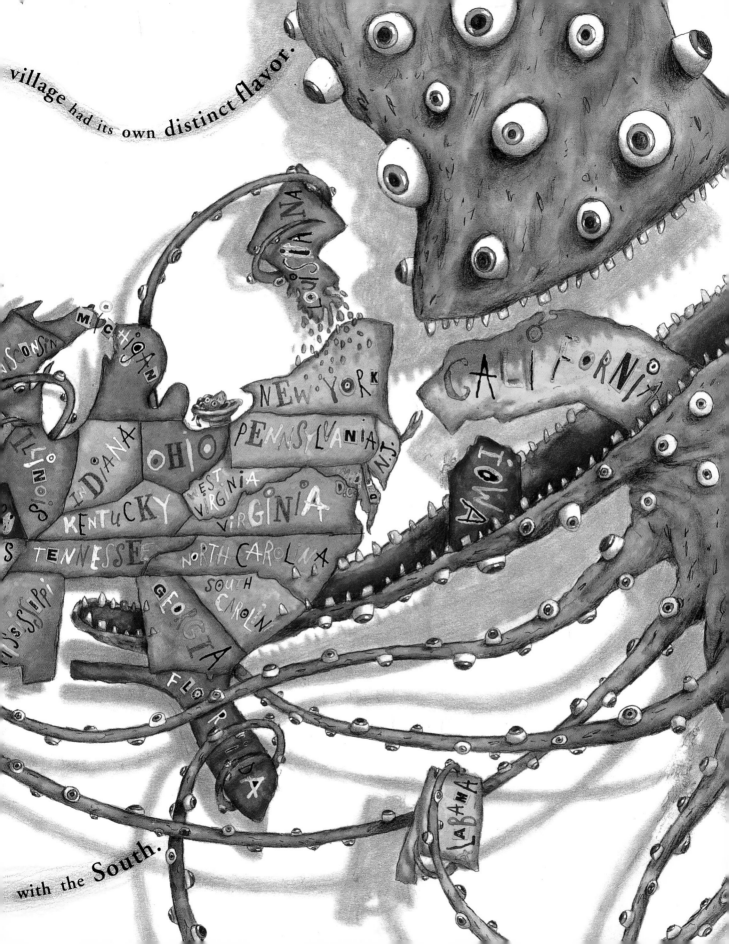

The **Rocky** Mountains he licked up like a **snow cone**

(WITH GRAVEL SPRINKLES)

(BURP!)

A nice **appetizer** he thought.

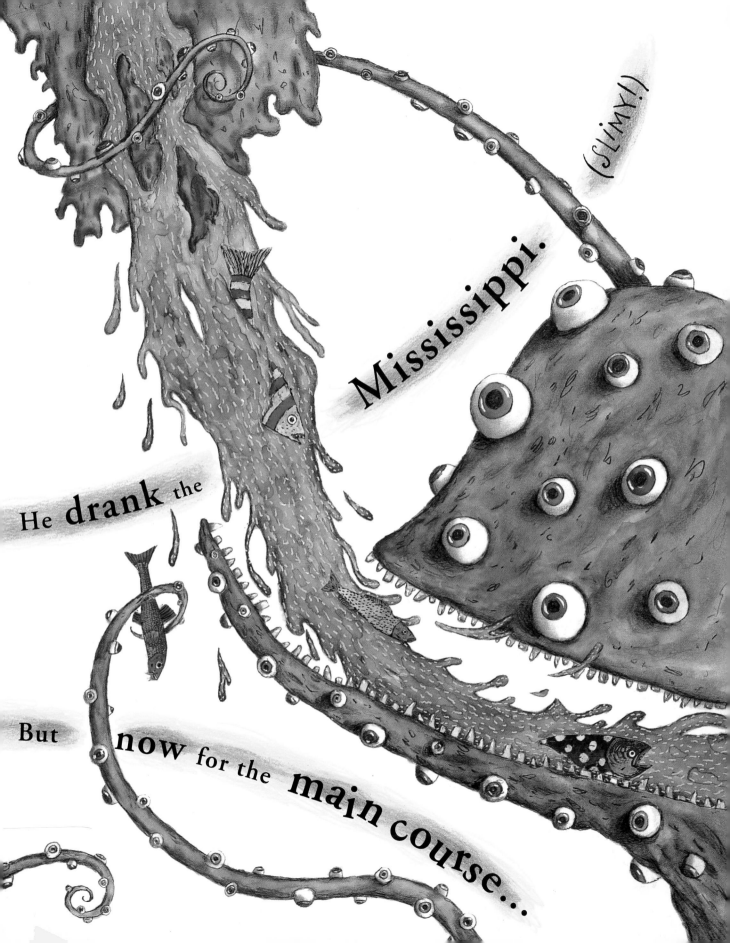

That was a job for a truly **monstrous belly!**

He turned himself into a

gigantic fire-breathing **tyrannosaurus rat** and proceeded to **gobble** up the earth like a **peeled orange**.

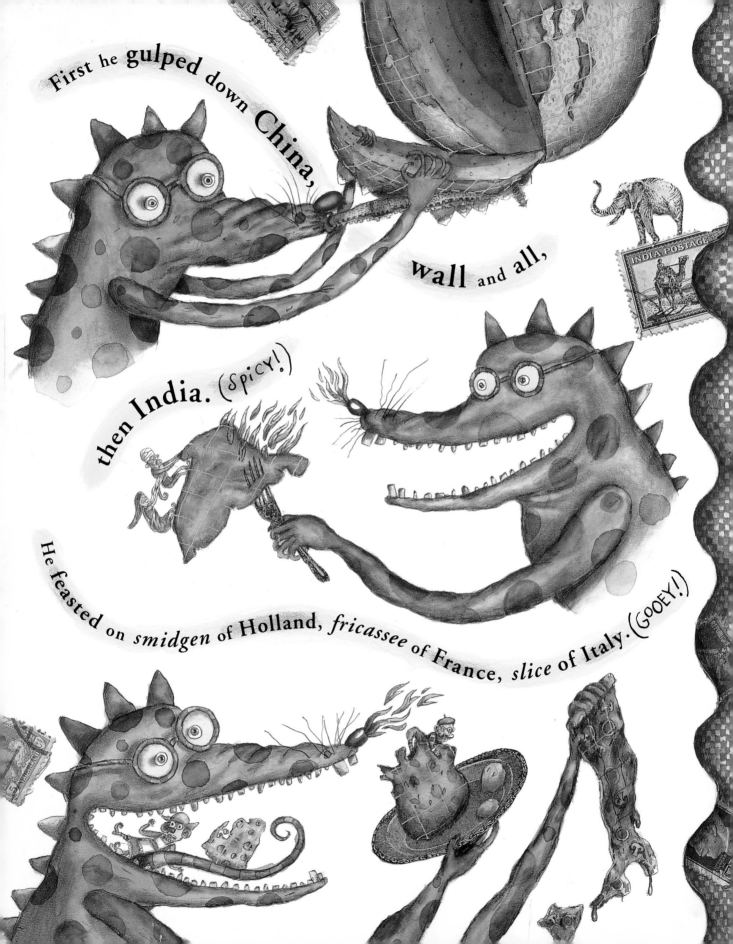

First he gulped down **China**, **wall** and all, then **India.** *(Spicy!)*

He feasted on *smidgen of Holland, fricassee of France, slice of Italy.* *(Gooey!)*

Around the world he **chomped**, and the smaller it got, the **fatter** he grew. Dessert was the South Pole.

For a midnight snack he rolled South America up in

Africa, swallowing them whole like an enchilada.

When he was done, there was **nothing** left of the **world**, which left him hanging Just him, the **moon**, and the plate of **string beans** and **cheese** soufflé With a **swift** swat of his tail, he sent the **dish** whirling from the **moon**.

...that he had eaten around.

...into s p a c e .

He dangled there for a **moment** or **two**. DIGESTING. STARGAZING. Passing the time (*AND SOME GAS!*). He felt **tired** and **lonesome**.

So he changed back into a **boy** named **Mo** and **poured** out **all** that was in the **huge belly**.

The countries, the rivers, the President, the towns, the people, his classmates, his teacher, his neighbors, their cat, First Lady, First Frog and First Dog, his best friend, Theo,

and *finally* his Mom and Dad, who were

It was decided that string beans and

Then they picked up Mo's best friend, Theo,

very **happy** to see their little **rapscallion** again.

cheese **soufflé** were **off** the menu **forever.**

and went **downtown** for **banana splits**

(WHICH IS A NICE WAY TO END A BUSY DAY).

Contents

Preface

Vintage Quilts
Identifying, Collecting, Dating, Preserving, and Valuing

This is a comprehensive guide to collecting antique quilts for the novice as well as the sophisticated and experienced collector. Quilt historians and appraisers Sharon Newman, Bobbie Aug, and Gerald Roy, curator of the prestigious Pilgrim/Roy collection, wrote this guide.

Age, pattern, style, size, fabrics, colors, construction techniques, and the quiltmaker and place of origin when available, are used to identify over 600 quilts, quilt tops, and blocks. A specific value or range is given for each. Quilt tops and blocks were included because we have observed a recent passion for collecting these in addition to quilts. Hopefully, you will discover a broad assortment of quilts, tops, and blocks that cover a wide range of values. You should find quilts that you see every day as well as those that are extremely rare and expensive.

It should be noted that all of the textiles in this book, except for two or three family quilts, were purchased by the authors. We shopped the retail market in our own vicinities, regionally, and nationally and made these purchases. We have experienced the values listed in these pages! However, since these quilts were all purchased over a long period of time, our over fifty cumulative years of professional quilt appraisal experience made it possible for us to ascertain current values for our textiles.

Each quilt, top, and block is pictured in color. Where helpful, we have indicated specific information about each item that collectors should find of interest.

Information is presented about structuring a comprehensive quilt collection. Suggestions for storage, display, preservation, and conservation are also included.

The values in this book are retail values and should be used only as a guide. They are not intended to set prices, which vary from one region of the country to another and are affected by the condition of the textile as well as supply and demand and the local and national economy. The only true guide to determining value is between a buyer and a seller. Neither the authors nor the publisher assume responsibility for any losses that might be incurred as a result of consulting this guide.

Introduction

Hundreds of thousands of quilts were made during the past two centuries by American quiltmakers. The need for warm covering was a motive for quiltmaking in the earliest times, but the beauty created by many of the quiltmakers has intrigued collectors for many years. Quilts of all patterns and styles continue to turn up in estate sales and regional auctions. The current interest in quiltmaking by a million and a half Americans has renewed a parallel interest in the quilts of the past. Interest in antique quilts has resulted in statewide quilt search days and the publication of state history and statistics about antique quilts. Fabrics and quilts designed from antique patterns are frequently published in magazines sold internationally.

During the past quarter century, American quilts have received recognition worldwide as the cultural and artistic value of quilts continues to be explored. Quilts can be purchased in many places. The flea market find is rare in this day of well-published information about all quilts, but bargains are still to be found in local auctions, estate sales, and antique stores. Vendors of antique quilts can be found in the many quilt shows throughout the country. Internet quilt dealers are plentiful and the quilts can be viewed at all times of the night and day.

Cover design: Beth Summers
Book design: Holly C. Long

COLLECTOR BOOKS
P.O. Box 3009
Paducah, Kentucky 42002-3009
www.collectorbooks.com

Copyright © 2002 Bobbie Aug, Sharon Newman, Gerald Roy

The current values in this book should be used only as a guide. They are not intended to set prices, which vary from one section of the country to another. Auction prices as well as dealer prices vary greatly and are affected by condition as well as demand. Neither the authors nor the publisher assumes responsibility for any losses that might be incurred as a result of consulting this guide.

Searching For A Publisher?

We are always looking for people knowledgeable within their fields. If you feel that there is a real need for a book on your collectible subject and have a large comprehensive collection, contact Collector Books.

VINTAGE Quilts

IDENTIFYING,
COLLECTING, DATING,
PRESERVING
&
VALUING

Bobbie Aug,
Sharon Newman
&
Gerald Roy

db
COLLECTOR BOOKS
A Division of Schroeder Publishing Co., Inc.